Leave it to

The Misadventures of a recycled Super Robot

2

Story and Art by
Kenji Sonishi

Leave It to PET Vol. 2

STORY & ART BY Kenji Sonishi

Translation/Katherine Schilling
Touch-up Art & Lettering/John Hunt
Cover & Book Design/Frances O. Liddell
Editor/Traci N. Todd

VP, Production/Alvin Lu
VP, Publishing Licensing/Rika Inouye
VP, Sales & Product Marketing/Gonzalo Ferreyra
VP, Creative/ Linda Espinosa
Publisher/Hyoe Narita

MAKASETE PET KUN Vol. 2

Printed in the U.S.A.

Published by VIZ Media, LLC
P.O. Box 77010
San Francisco, CA 94107

10 9 8 7 6 5 4 3 2 1
First printing, July 2009

www.vizkids.com

Contents:

PET's Haiku p.6

CHAPTER 1 Return of the Can Crew! p.7
CHAPTER 2 A Mysterious Gadget p.15
CHAPTER 3 The Dynamite Punch! p.23
CHAPTER 4 Go Fetch! p.35

CHAPTER 5 The Unbearable Lightness of P-2 p.47
CHAPTER 6 Meet L'il Bagz! p.53
CHAPTER 7 I'll Form the Head! p.65
CHAPTER 8 Tin, Inc. p.77

CHAPTER 9 The PET Catcher p.83
CHAPTER 10 It's a Race! p.95
CHAPTER 11 Let's Work Together! p.107
CHAPTER 12 Meet Five Cups! p.113

CHAPTER 13 Five Kinds of Help p.125
CHAPTER 14 Plaz About the House p.137
CHAPTER 15 The Haunted House p.143
CHAPTER 16 Let's Get Out of Here! p.155

CHAPTER 17 A Day with PET p.167
CHAPTER 18 The Haunted School p.173

PET's Special Bonus Tracks! p.185

The Story **A plastic bottle gets recycled and comes back as a helpful robot!**

Meet Noboru, your average Japanese elementary school student. One day he finds a plastic bottle in the park and recycles it. Then the bottle comes back as the robot "**PET**"! **PET** can transform, combine with other robots, and use special **PET** gadgets! Together with his sister, **Alu**, and friend, **Plaz**, **PET** saves Noboru from all kinds of trouble...at least, that's the idea.

Who's Who

Bottle Doggie
Recycled from:
Mini Plastic Bottle
PET
Recycled from:
An Orange Plastic Bottle
Alu
Recycled from:
A Cola Can
The Can Crew
Often mistaken
Recycled from:
Coffee Cans
Galvin
Wootz
COFFEE
COFFEE
Recycler
Noboru Ogawara

PET's Haiku*

YOU CAN SORT IT, BUT
IF IT'S OUT ON THE WRONG DAY
IT'S ONLY GARBAGE.

*A haiku is a type of Japanese poem that is three lines long. The first line has five syllables, the second has seven, and the third has five again.

CHAPTER 1 Return of the Can Crew!

GALVIN
CAN CREW BOSS

WOOTZ
CAN CREW MEMBER

BOTH WERE BORN WHEN NOBORU OGAWARA, AGE 82, RECYCLED SOME TIN COFFEE CANS!

CHAPTER 1

Return of the Can Crew!

HA! VIDEO
THE PUPPET MASTER
VIDEO
PET
THAT VIDEO YOU RENTED!
HERE!
THANKS!
The P-Master! Cool!
YOU REWOUND THIS, RIGHT?
WHA--?!
UM, YEAH!
NOBORU YAMADA, AGE 9.
POP
THE PUPPET MASTER VHS
NO YOU DIDN'T!
Not even a little!
HUH? OH, REALLY?

NEED A TAPE REWOUND?!
LEAVE IT TO *US*!!!

SO?
WHAT ?!

NOW, YOU'RE GONNA LET US HELP YOU *OR ELSE.*
WELL, WHEN YOU PUT IT THAT WAY...
BE MY GUEST.
ON SECOND THOUGHT, MAYBE I SHOULD JUST REWIND IT MYSELF–
VWIP
HUH ?!
NOT SO FAST!
WHAAAT ?!
ZING

KERCHNK
NOW !!!
BEGIN RE-WIND ...

LOOK, GUYS, I DON'T NEED ANY–
Oh yeah!
I'M THE ONE HELPING HIM, NOT YOU!!

IF IT WAS THAT EASY, WHY DIDN'T YOU JUST DO IT?!
GRRR
WHIRR
HEH HEH !
COFFEE

THUD
WRECK-ING BALL!

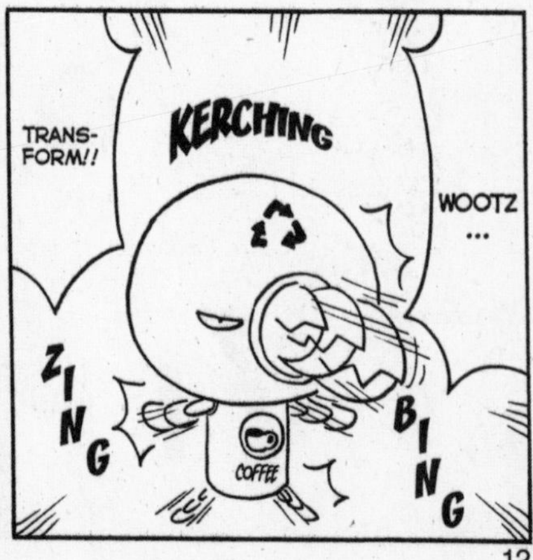
TRANS-FORM!!
KERCHING
WOOTZ ...
ZING
BING
COFFEE

BONK
WHOA! YOU'RE NOT KIDDING AROUND!

CATCH
VWIP
GALVIN, NOW!!!

PLUNK

DONE!
UM, THANKS...
ZUP
WOW, quick!

REWIND!
REWIND!!!
ZING
ZING
WHIR
RRRRRR
COFFEE

ALU, ATTACK!!!
!!
ZONK

HERE, PET!
TOSS
CATCH
THANKS!

KACHUNK

FAST FORWARD, GO!!!
WHIRRR
AH HA HA
Grrr!
ARGH! JUST GIVE IT BACK!!!

CHAPTER 2
A Mysterious Gadget
The Lady Alu
Master PET
RESCUE
CRAYONS

RECYCLING CENTER
PET RECREATIONAL ROOM
VROOM
SCREECH
RUMMAGE RUMMAGE
RUMMAGE RUMMAGE

PET!
WHAT'S THIS DO?
HUH ...?!
WHAT'S WHAT DO?

WHOA! WHAT'S THAT?

WHAT DO YOU MEAN? ISN'T IT YOURS?
BOING
HUH?! I'VE NEVER SEEN IT!
BOING

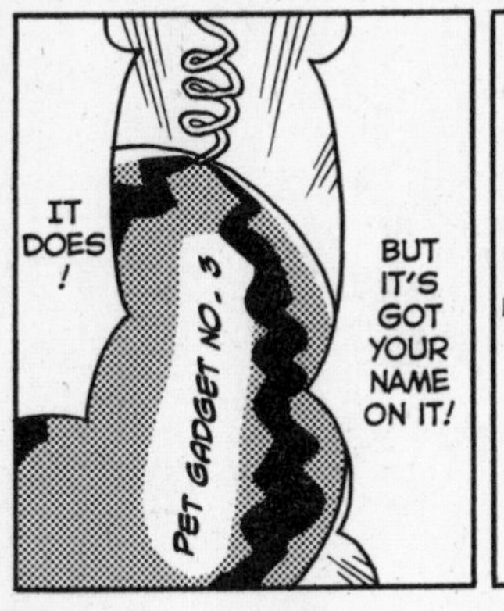
BUT IT'S GOT YOUR NAME ON IT!
IT DOES!
PET GADGET NO. 3

HUH...I GUESS I DID HAVE ONE OF THESE.
WHERE WAS IT?
BOING
BOING
BEHIND THE RIBBIT HAT!

WELL, IT'S A MYSTERY TO ME!
KLAK
I'M GONNA GO ASK MR. SHIMADA!
OK!

BOING
BOING

BEEP
BEEP
BEEP
PET
UWEEEEN
CLINK
FINALLY!
VWEEEEN

Gadget Design
EXCUSE ME.
WHAT'S THIS?

RECYCLING CENTER GADGET DESIGN
Gadget Design
Reduce garbage together!
Garbage Production Levels
AH, IT'S PET!
TESTING
TEST GADGET
BOING
BOING

UH, THAT? THAT'S THE, ER, BOING BOING...
MR. SHIMADA LEAD CREATOR GADGET DESIGN
...
WAIT, THE BOING BOING WHAT?
HUH?
Boing Boing?

OH! "BOIINN-NNG!"
MR. MORITA SECTION CHIEF GADGET DESIGN
YEAH, THAT'S RIGHT!
THE BOING BOING BOIINNNG!
Design
Sorry about that!
? ?
...
HOW DO YOU USE IT ?!
BOING
BOING
AH, WELL ...
FIRST YOU OPEN THE HATCH ON YOUR HEAD UNIT...
CLACK
FIND THE A JACK ...
INSERT, AND LOCK!
KER
CHAK

BOINNNNG
DING
FWAP
BOING

NOW WAVE YOUR HEAD UP AND DOWN!
AND ?!

WOW! THAT'S A BLAST FROM THE PAST!
...
BOING
BOINNNG
DONK
DONK
THAT WAS ONE OF OUR FIRST CREATIONS. I REMEMBER— WE WERE EATING WATERMELON AT THAT PIÑATA PARTY...

BOINNNG
ZING
BOINNG
DONG
DING
....

KRAK
DING
I WANNA TRY!
ZING
BOINNNG
BOINNNG
....

PET! HELP ME!
No fair! I want a turn!
...
ZING
BOINNNG
BOINNNG
KRAK
HE'S TOTALLY INTO IT.

CHAPTER 3 The Dynamite Punch!

CHAPTER 3

The Dynamite Punch!

Cola

TESTING ROOM
RECYCLING CENTER

ALL RIGHT! HAVE AT IT, PET!
MR. SHIMADA GADGET DESIGN
Good luck, PET!
GULP
DYNAMITE PUNCH!!!
ZAKOOO

BOING
BOING
BOING

BOING
BOING
BOING
...
KRAK

ZINNNN
G
SUCCESS!
WHOA !!!
THAT WAS COOL!

TMP TMP TMP
DYNAMITE !!!
ZING
ZING
DYNAMITE !!!
I want a try!
PET !!!

OH, I'VE GOT SOMETHING NEW FOR YOU TOO, ALU!
REALLY ?! WHAT?
HERE!
THE SQUEAKY HAMMER!

WHOA!

WOBBLE
?!

WOBBLE
WOBBLE

TMP TMP TMP
TMP TMP TMP
AUGH !!

WACK
TH

ANOTHER SUCCESS!
Yippie!
GAH
...

BLOOP
BLOOP
PET!
EMERGENCY!
EMERGENCY!

PET, THEY NEED YOU!
BOOP
BOOP
BOOP
BOOP
SHIMADA
ROGER!

I'M OFF!!!
VWOON
VWOON
VWOON
WOOHOOOOO!

I'LL GO TOO!!
Woohoooo!
SCRAPE
SCRAPE
WOOHOOOOO!
GOOD LUCK!
RECYCLING CENTER

OH, SORRY. YOU WON'T NEED THOSE.
REALLY ...
BUMMED

OKAY, HERE'S THE DEAL.
I GOTTA WRITE A BOOK REPORT...
SO READ THIS BOOK, AND WRITE WHAT YOU THINK HERE–

OKAY, HOLD ON TIGHT!
Here goes!
GO FOR IT!
W-W-WAIT!!!

WHAT'RE YOU DOING?!
OH, NOTHING.
FWIP

ARE YOU LISTENING TO ME?!
NO! I MEAN YES!

DAAAA
I NEED HELP WITH THIS! IT'S A BOOK!
A CAT OF FLANDERS
MASTERPIECES OF WORLD LITERATURE
A CAT OF FLANDERS
A BOOK!
TA

RRIP
OK!!!
A CAT OF FLANDERS
BONK
ONE TWO!

AAAAARGH!!!
WAP
ALRIGHT!

CHAPTER 4

Go Fetch!

SCHOOL
BONG
BONG
STUDIES
JAPANESE
RUSTLE
RUSTLE
OH NO!
IT'S NOT HERE!
RUMMAGE
RUMMAGE
NOBORU YAMADA, AGE 9.
MUSIC
MATH
I PULLED AN ALL-NIGHTER TO WRITE THAT BOOK REPORT...
AND I FORGOT TO BRING IT!
WHAT—?!

WHAT DO I DO?!

YOU COULD GET PET TO BRING IT!
I'M SURE HE CAN DO THAT, CAN'T HE?
I DUNNO...

I THINK I LEFT IT ON MY DESK...
MAYBE HE *COULD* GET IT...

OK!
PET! HELP ME!!!

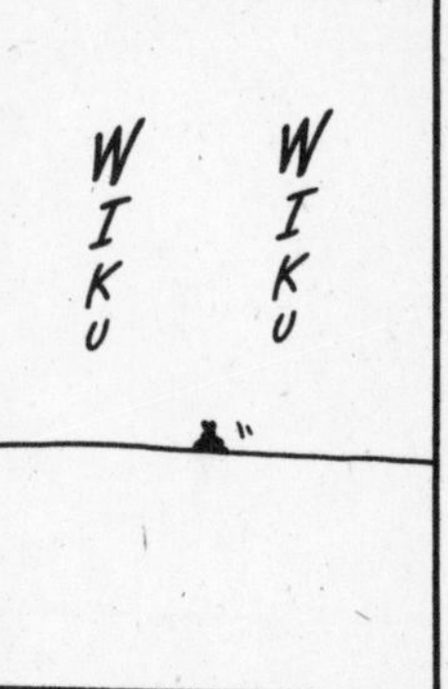
WIKU
WIKU

WIKU
WIKU

WIKU
WIKU
WIKU
WIKU

PET, REPORT-ING!!!
MUTTER MUTTER
THAT TOOK FOR-EVER!!!

WHY ARE YOU A TANK TODAY OF ALL DAYS!
I'M READY TO FIGHT !!!

I DON'T NEED YOU TO FIGHT! I NEED YOU TO RUN!!!
NO PROB-LEM!
See...

OBSERVE MY PET TREADS !!!

SQUEEEEK
THEY CAN CRAWL ACROSS ANY SURFACE !!!
WIKU
WIKU
WIKU
WIKU
Wow!
WHOA!!

OK, FINE! THIS IS WHAT I NEED YOU TO DO!
UH HUH
UH HUH
IT'S EASY, SO LISTEN UP!

I NEED YOU TO BRING ME THE BOOK REPORT ON MY DESK AT HOME!
OK?
Can you remember that?
NOD

IT'S ON MY DESK!!!
ROGER!

WIKU
WIKU
WIKU
WOW!!!

WOK

THUNK

VWEEEN
ARGH! SO LAME!

THANK YOU!
Bye!
WIKU
WIKU
NOW I'M WORRIED.

VWIP
VWIP
OK... ON THE DESK...

WHAT DID NOBORU NEED?

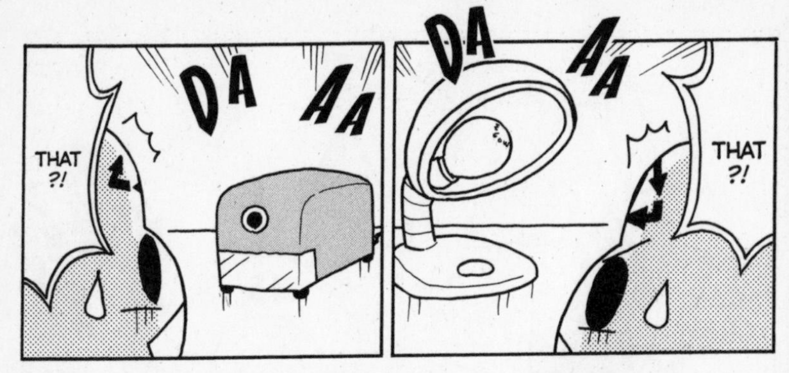
DA
AA
THAT ?!
DA
AA
THAT ?!

UM ...?!

ZIG
WHAT WAS IT?!
WHAT WAS IT?!
ZAG

HUH ?!
STEP ASIDE! WE'LL HELP!!!

THE CAN CREW ?!
KRASH

WE'LL TAKE THAT BOOK REPORT!!!
NO !!!

SNIK
MWA HA HA !!!
NICE TRY, BUT THAT'S NOT IT.

PET'S TAKING TOO LONG ...
MY TURN'S COMING SOON!

VERY GOOD!
THUNK
NEXT REPORT... NOBORU, PLEASE!

UM, PRES-ENT!
I'M DOOMED!

I MADE IT!!!
TA
DA
PET!!!

KA
HERE!
THUNK

THONK
Woo hoo!
Argh!!!

CHAPTER 5

The Unbearable Lightness of P-2

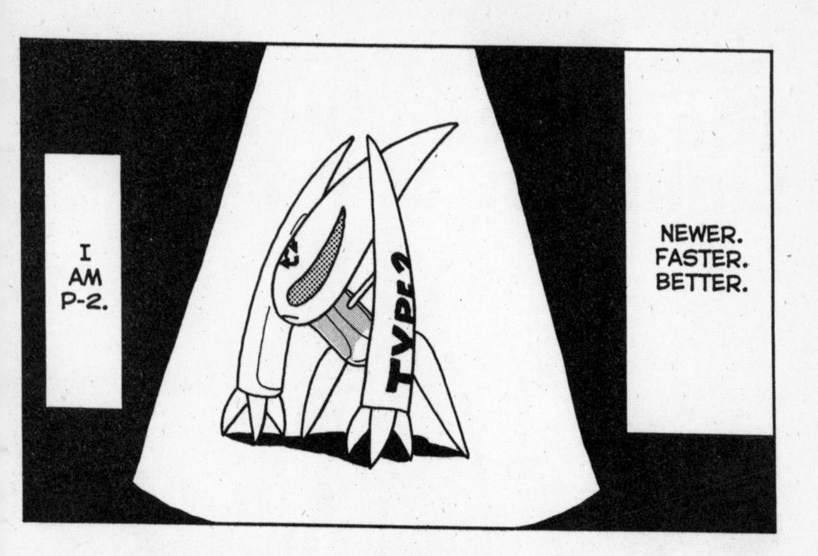
NEWER.
FASTER.
BETTER.
I AM P-2.
TYPE2

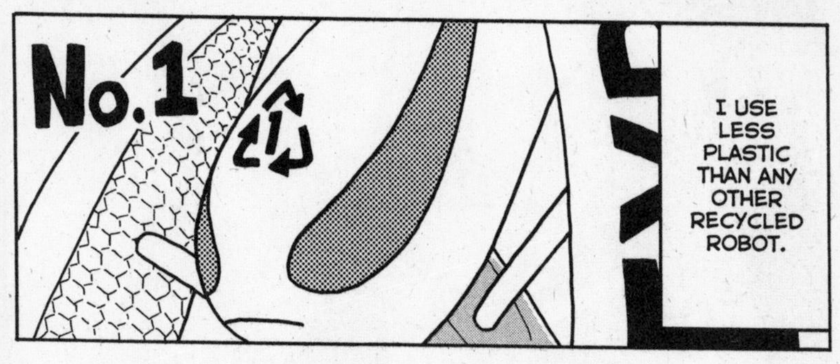
I USE LESS PLASTIC THAN ANY OTHER RECYCLED ROBOT.
No.1

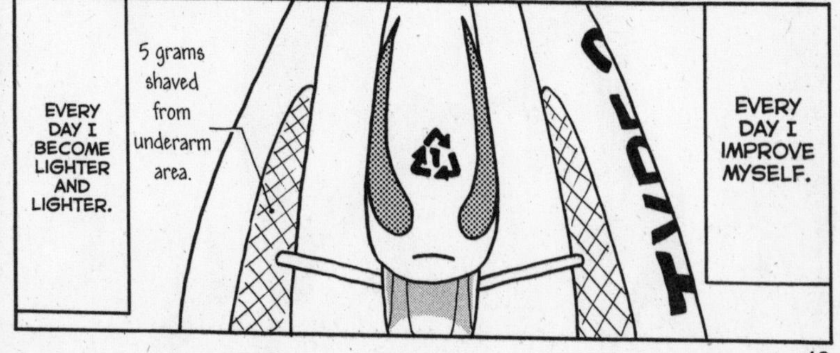
EVERY DAY I IMPROVE MYSELF.
EVERY DAY I BECOME LIGHTER AND LIGHTER.
5 grams shaved from underarm area.

UNTIL AUTOMATIC DOORS WON'T OPEN FOR ME.
. . . . .
AUTOMATIC

I AM P-2.
TYPE

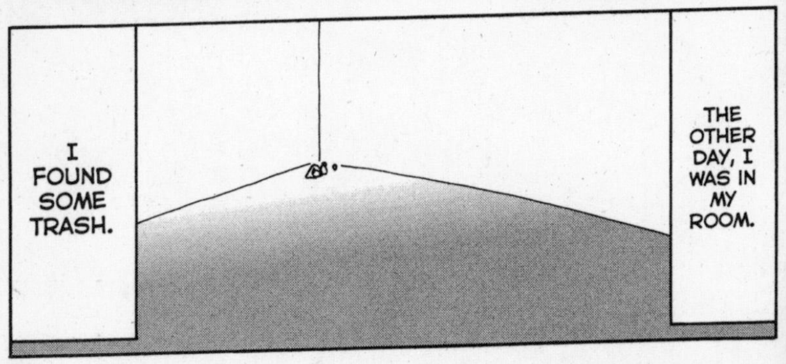
THE OTHER DAY, I WAS IN MY ROOM.
I FOUND SOME TRASH.

I TRIED TO VACUUM IT UP.
VWOOOON
THE VACUUM SUCKED ME UP INSTEAD.

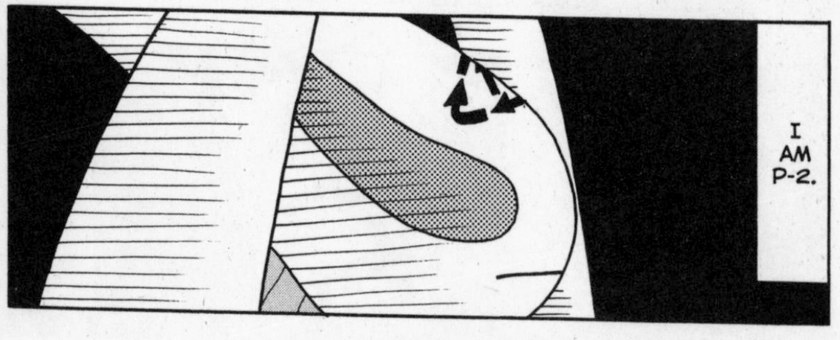
I AM P-2.

I TOOK A WALK IN TOWN.
WIN PRIZES!!
FUN!
A LADY GAVE ME A BALLOON.

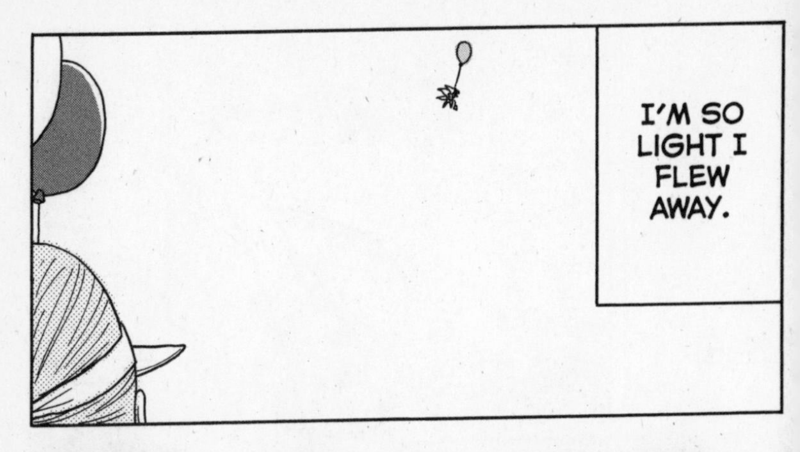
I'M SO LIGHT I FLEW AWAY.

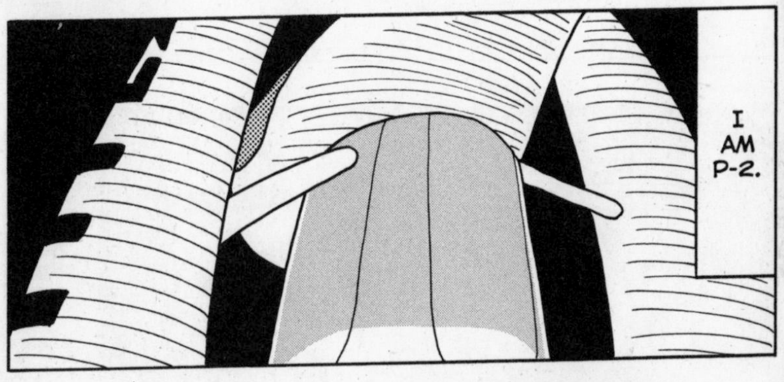
I AM P-2.

NOBORU NEEDS HELP.
HEEEELLLLP
I SHOULD GO.

BUT IT'S TOO WINDY. I'LL STAY HOME INSTEAD.

I AM P-2.

I AM P-2 ...

I AM P-2 ...

SOME-TIMES, I GET STUCK UNDER TOWELS AND CAN'T MOVE.
Wow, tough.
Maybe you're too light?
I AM P-2.

CHAPTER 6

Meet L'il Bagz!

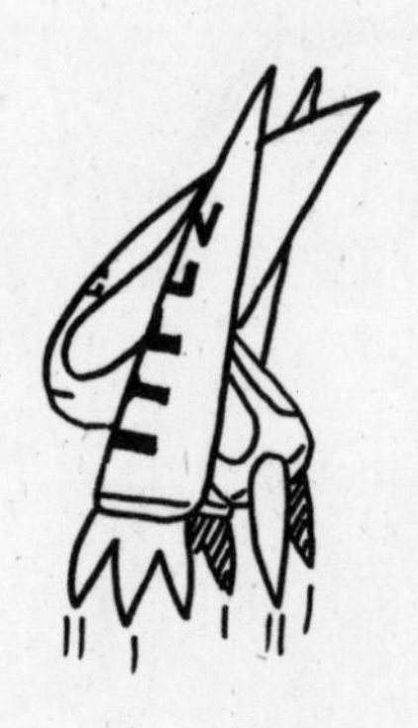

VWIP
VWIP
VWIP
VWIP
FOUND IT!
WAIT... THAT'S NOT IT.
NOBORU YAMADA, AGE 9.
Milk Caramels
Milk Caramels
JUST GARBAGE!
I DON'T BELIEVE IT!
TOSS
I'LL NEVER FIND THAT GAME...
PET!!!!

TA DAAA
I'M PET! NOBORU'S FAITHFUL ALLY!
I'M PET! NOBOWU'S FAIFOO AWWAI!

NO, I'M PET!
You forgot ?!
OH. WIGHT!
HUH...?

READY? ONE, TWO ...

What was my name again?
WHAT'S GOING ON?!

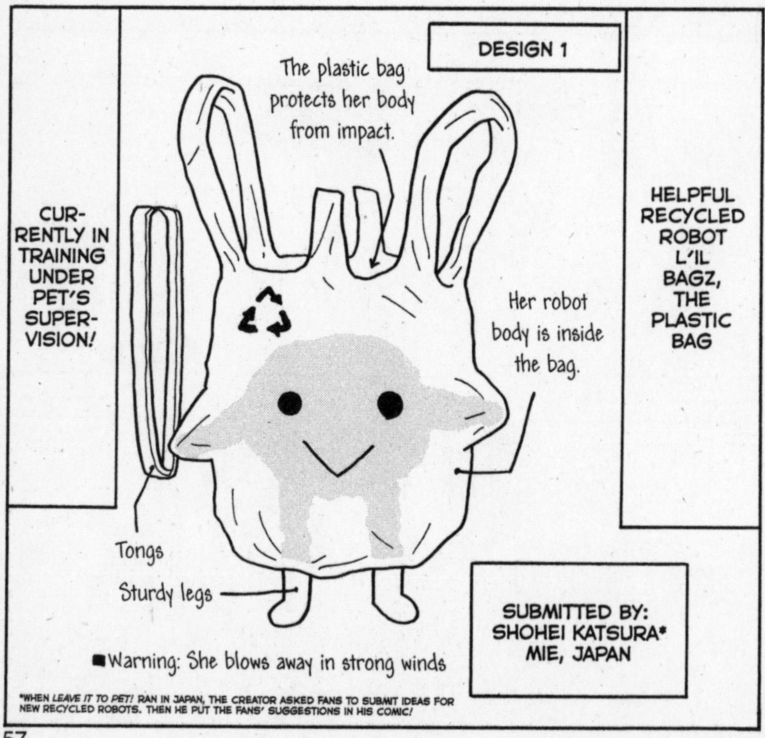

*WHEN *LEAVE IT TO PET!* RAN IN JAPAN, THE CREATOR ASKED FANS TO SUBMIT IDEAS FOR NEW RECYCLED ROBOTS. THEN HE PUT THE FANS' SUGGESTIONS IN HIS COMIC!

I'LL BE WATCHING FROM OVER HERE! GOOD LUCK!
You can do it!
I CAN DWOO IT!
EH ?!

S-SO WHAT DO I DO?
JUST ASK HER TO DO SOME-THING!

OH, OK.
UM, L'IL BAGZ?
I DROPPED A GAME AROUND HERE. CAN YOU FIND IT?

LIKE THAT?
Wet's find it!
OK! OK!

NO PWOB-WEM!

SPESHUL W'IL BAGZ GADGET!!!

ZOIK

FOUND IT!!!
WHAT ?

RUSTLE
RUSTLE
...
...

MELON
SODA
10%

UM, THAT'S NOT IT.
Not at all.
WONG?

ZZUP

HUH ?!
OH, NO!
SNIFF
SNIFF

IT'S OK...
YOU CAN DO IT!

HMPH !
WH- WHAT?
Did I say something?

WHAT'S WRONG WITH THIS?!!
See?
MELON SODA
EVERY- THING !!!

LET'S LOOK TOGETHER, OK?
C'mon, please?
JUST ONE MORE TIME!

YOU JUST DON'T GET IT !!!
HUH —?!
Get what ?!

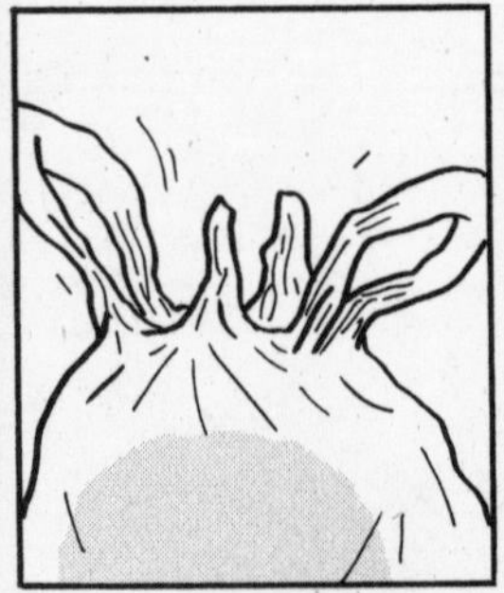

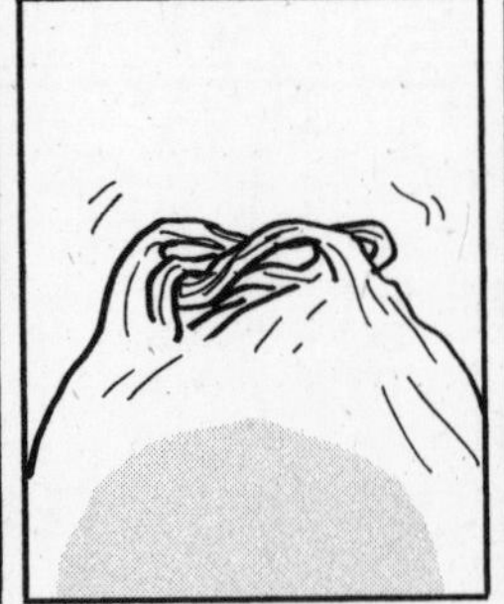

OK!
Wet's do it!
ATTA GIRL!
WHEW ...

OK! HERE GOES!!!
WOOOO!

RUSTLE
RUSTLE
PAT
PAT

WHAT WERE WE LOOKING FOR AGAIN?

KA
THUMP
OK!
Let's sort it!
KLINK KLINK

CHAPTER 7

I'll Form the Head!

HEY!
COOL! LET'S DO IT!
I KNOW A SHORTCUT!
NOBORU YAMADA, AGE 9.
HIROTA, AGE 9.
SNAG
ACK!
OK! KEEP UP!
YOU BET!

ARGH! I'M CAUGHT!
LEMME LOOK AT IT!
LET'S SEE...

NO GOOD! I CAN'T GET IT OFF!
IT'S ALL TANGLED UP!
WAIT, I KNOW!

PET !!!

PET HEAD, REPORTING!!!
VWOOOO

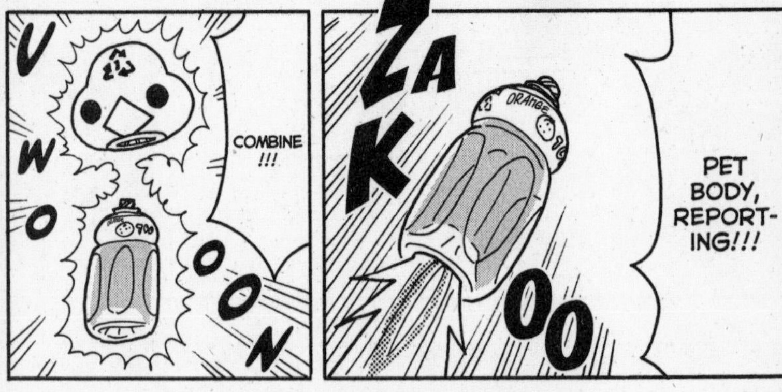
PET BODY, REPORTING!!!
ZAK
OO
COMBINE!!!
VWOOOON

KER
CHING

PET, REPORTING!!!
TADAA
WHAT THE HECK?!

ACK! I FORGOT MY ARMS AND LEGS!
ZAKIIIN
THAT'S NOT WHAT I MEANT!!!
SO, WHAT'S THE PROBLEM?
YOU, FOR ONE!!!
TOK TOK TOK

AH HA! YOU'RE STUCK!
Hmm. I see, I see...
THINK YOU CAN GET ME LOOSE?

I'M NOT SURE I CAN DO ANYTHING LIKE THIS!
WHOSE FAULT IS THAT?!

OR LIKE THIS!
UGH, HOPE-LESS!
Back to normal
OK, TIME TO CALL FOR SUPPORT!
SUP-PORT?

TA DA !!!
THUNK
OVER HERE!
ALU IS YOUR SUPPORT ?!
She's upside down too?!

DONK
GO, PET, GO!!
YAY! YAY! GO, PET, GO!
FWEE FWEE
DONK
THAT'S NOT THE KIND OF SUPPORT WE NEED!!!

ALU! COMBINE !!!
COMBINE ...?
ROGER !

CAN'T YOU TWO WORK TOGETHER OR SOME-THING?
THAT'S RIGHT!

ZINN
GNN
ORANGE 100
ZING
Cola
ORANGE 100
SHHUP
CHING
POK
UWOO
NNN
KAZING
Cola

PETALU, REPORTING!!
TA DAA
PET's head
Alu's hands
PET's legs
PETALU ?!

STAGGER

NO! NO! TO THE RIGHT!
WHERE? HERE?
Alu can't see a thing.

THAT'S THE STUPIDEST THING I'VE EVER SEEN!!!
YOU WERE BETTER APART!!!
OK, ALU!
TRANS-FORM !!!
It's like the blind leading the blind...

ALUPET, REPORT-ING!!!
Alu's head
Pet's hands
Alu's legs
Alupet ?!
HOW IS THIS ANY DIFFER-ENT?!

UM, WHICH WAY WAS RIGHT?
Hurry!
WAAAAAH!
ZING

PLAZ, REPORT-ING!
PLAZ! THANK GOOD-NESS!

NOOOOO!
HUH? COM-BINE?

SOB
PLAZPETALU
ZUD
ZUD
ZUD

TINY TIN!
ALL DONE!
PAT
PAT
SNIP
SNIP
SNIP
SNIP

...
THUNK

VWOOSH
ARGH! I HATE THAT GUY!
How does he do it?!
I HATE HIM TOO!!!

CHAPTER 8

Tin, Inc.

TINY
TIN.
RECYCLED
ROBOT...
AND
BUSINESS
MAN.
MORNING
COFFEE

MORNING.
Tin, Inc.
TIN
HE
GOES
TO THE
OFFICE.

KLAK
GOOD
MORN-
ING!

HEAD OF
THE COMPANY
WE MISSED YOU!
WELCOME BACK!
SECRETARY
CLERK
DIRECTOR
SECTION CHIEF
MANAGER

HOW DID YOUR JOB GO?!

TOK
TOK
TOK
FIRST, TINY TIN REPORTS TO THE MANAGER.

THE MANAGER REPORTS TO THE SECTION CHIEF.
KNOCK
KNOCK
I SAVED NOBORU FROM A WIRE FENCE!
Manager ← Tiny Tin
GREAT!
MORNING COFFEE
THE SECTION CHIEF REPORTS TO THE DIRECTOR.
KNOCK KNOCK
WE ATE STEW AND PIES OF MINCE!
Section Chief ← Manager
EXCEL-LENT!
THE DIRECTOR REPORTS TO THE CLERK.
KNOCK KNOCK
WHEN SHAVING, DON'T FORGET TO RINSE!
Director ← Section Chief
IMPRESSIVE!

THE CLERK REPORTS TO THE ADMINISTRATIVE ASSISTANT.
KNOCK KNOCK
EH–?!
Clerk ← Director
TINY TIN'S A SHINY PRINCE!

RIGHT... RIGHT!
HUM DUM LA DEE DAH.

YES?
BOSS! I HAVE TODAY'S REPORT!
THE SECRETARY REPORTS TO THE HEAD OF THE COMPANY.
TOK TOK
OK THEN.

WE NEED MORE LLAMAS!

STAMP
APPROVED!

GOOD WORK, TINY TIN!
WHAT THE-?!

NICE WORK!
ANOTHER DAY IN THE LIFE OF TINY TIN.
ALRIGHT!
We need more llamas!
APPROVED

CHAPTER 9 The PET Catcher

CHAPTER 9

The PET Catcher

VROOOO
OOOOM

ALRIGHT! I WON AGAIN!
TIME TO SET A NEW RECORD!

PEAK RACER 2
THEY AREN'T LETTING US HAVE A TURN AT ALL!
I gotta go home at 4...
TRY CALLING PET!

RIGHT!
PET !!!

HI THERE.
FOUR KINDS IN ALL!
THE ANIMALS
ZOIK

PET?!
YO! NOBORU! WHAT UP?!
WHAT ARE YOU DOING IN THERE?!

UM...
GOOD QUESTION.
I KINDA GOT STUCK IN HERE.

CAN YOU GET ME OUT?
Please ...?
WHA -?!
700円
500円

YOU KNOW I'M BROKE!
CHING
Thanks!

OK! A little further!
UWEEN

VWEEEN
SNIK

WOW.
YOU
STINK!
WHA
-?!

GRRR!
WATCH
THIS!
KLANK

OK!
THERE
WE GO!
SNIK
VWEEEN

GRRR
KK

SLIP

VWEEEN
AW! TOO BAD !!!
YOU LITTLE--!

TRY HELPING NEXT TIME!
OH, RIGHT!
GRRR !!!
Good luck!
KLANK

NOT YET... NOT YET!
VWEEEN
THERE! STOP!!!

BOINK
UNFF.

GRRRRK
AL-
RIGHT
!!!
KLANK

SPOK

YOUR HEAD CAME OFF!!!
ZOMG

YOUR PRIZE
DOK

SO CLOSE!!
SO CLOSE? I RIPPED YOUR HEAD OFF!!!
DINK

OK, NOBORU! GO FOR THE NARROW PART OF THE BOTTLE!!!
I KNOW, I KNOW!!!
VWEEN

GAK
YES!!
ORANGE 100

ZZZ
POK
ORANGE 100

NO WONDER I COULDN'T PICK IT UP!
VWEEEEN
Keep coming... More...

YOUR PRIZE
THUNK

ALRIGHT!!
WE DID IT!!!

MY WORK HERE IS DONE!
Boy, I'm good.
NOT SO FAST!!!

CHAPTER 10

It's a Race!

WHAT?!
THEY WON'T TAKE TURNS?!

YEAH...
PEAK RACER 2
Awesome!
VROOOM
LEAVE IT TO ME!
Hold this for me.

PET, TRANS-FORM!
SHAPE OF: ARCADE EMPLOYEE!
TA
DAAAAN
ZUP
RATTLE

TA DAA!
ARCADE EMPLOYEE.
UM, YOU JUST PUT ON A TIE.

EXCUSE ME, SIR.
TAP
TAP
TAP
HUH ?

WAH! YOU AGAIN ?
KLAK
KLAK

POK

POP

ZZZT
HEY! WHAT'RE YOU DOING?!

SNX
ROADSTER
PET REPORT-ING!!!
TA DAAA!

WHOA! WHAT'S GOING ON?!
HA HA HA HA
HUH ?!
WAAAH
WHO'S HE?!

PET, TRANS-FORM!
FORM OF: P-1 RACER!

DING
Propeller
Rubber band
Racing Tires
P-1 RACER

I'LL TAKE YOU ON!
WHA-?!
PET! ARE YOU CRAZY?!

ZING
IF YOU LOSE, YOU STOP PLAYING!

FINE!
HEY! I GET IT!

AND IF I WIN?!
HUH?!

I'LL... GIVE YOU YOUR MONEY BACK!
YOU'RE ON!
OH NO!!!

VROOM
3...
Easy!
2...
GULP
1...
VROOM
WIKU
WIKU
START
!!!
SKREEEEECH
VROOM

ZAZOOM

FINISH
I DID IT!
I WON!

ZUK
EH?!

2nd
FINISH
VROOM
SOME-ONE WIND ME UP !!!
NOW'S MY CHANCE!
I DON'T BELIEVE IT!!!

VROOM
TOO BAD, LOSER!!
ARGH!

SM
AK
THERE YOU GO, PET!
THANKS, ALU!

WIND
WIND
WIND
YOU TOO, PLAZ!

ZOOM

ALRIGHT! I WON!!!
SMACK
THAT'S SO NOT FAIR!!!

Grr...
OK! Our turn!
Right on!
Way to go, PET!
...

CHAPTER 11

Let's Work Together!

YO, NOBORU! WHAT'S THAT?!
HIROTA, AGE 9.
NOBORU YAMADA, AGE 9.
YOSHIKAWA, AGE 9.
EH?!
ZUD
ZUD
ZUD

ZUD
ZUD
ZUD
ZUD

WHOA!
ZUD
ZUD
ZUD
ZUD
LOOK AT ALL OF 'EM!

HOW CAN WE HELP YOU TODAY?!
WHA–?!

UH, UM, I'M NOT SURE... YET.
Gimme some time, guys...

OK! WE'LL JUST HAVE TO DECIDE OUR-SELVES!
UM ...

ZZUK
ZING
KER
CHAK
DING
ZUP
ZUP
ZUP
INTRO-DUCING...
TA
DAAA
THE PET UNICYCLE!!!

NOW, THINK OF SOMETHING I CAN DO TO HELP USING THIS!
WOBBLE
WOBBLE
WHA-? WHY?!

WE'RE WAITING!!!
VWIP
VWIP
VWIP
VWIP
COFFEE
COFFEE
MORNING COFFEE
VWIP
VWIP
VWIP
VWIP
VWIP
ALL OF YOU?!

GUYS, I REALLY CAN'T THINK OF ANYTHING ...
UM, HOW ABOUT YOU CARRY MY BACKPACK?
HEAR THAT? GO, TEAM !!!
YEAH!

UP! UP!
UP!
THIS IS SO EMBAR-RASSING...

NOT TO MENTION SLOW.
OUR SCHOOL
Hurry it up!
C'mon, Noboru!

CHAPTER 12

Meet Five Cups!

KER
SPLASH
NOBORU YAMADA, AGE 9.
What do I do?!
OH NO! I DROPPED MY GAME IN A PUDDLE!
YIPES!
DRIP
DRIP
ZZZAAAP
HAVE YOU TRIED TURNING IT ON?
...OK!
KLIK

NOTHING!
WOW...
KLIK
KLIK
NOT EVEN A BLEEP!
CAN PET HELP ...?

IT'S WORTH A TRY!
ONE, AND-A-
PET! HELP US!!!
TINK

I HEAR THE CALL AND I COME!
I'M PET!

KER
SPLASH
.....

WHA —?!
You're kidding!
WHAK
WHAK
NOT EVEN A BLEEP!
I THOUGHT PET HAD WATER IN HIS BOTTLE ...

UNNNH

WHAT ABOUT THE OTHER ROBOTS?
I'VE NEVER TRIED CALLING THEM.

WELL, NO TIME LIKE THE PRESENT!
TINY TIN!!!
ALU!!!
PLAZ!!!

. . . . .
NOTH-
ING.
NOTH-
ING.

WHO ELSE IS THERE?
UM
...
P-2!!!
CAN CREW!!!
L'IL BAGZ
!!!

. . . . .
NOT A ONE...
YEAH
...
I'M STARTING TO WONDER HOW THIS EVER WORKS.

SOMEONE COME! WE DON'T CARE WHO!!!

TINK
L-
LOOK!
WHAT
?!
HUH
...

WHIZZ
WHIZZ
WHIZZ
WHIZZ

DO
K

HIROTA!!!
WE PAPER CUPS ARE HERE TO HELP YOU!
1
HIROTA
WHA-?! ME?
No way!
TA DAAA

DID YOU RECYCLE A PAPER CUP?
I DON'T REMEMBER...
WHAT DOES HE MEAN "CUPS"? THERE'S ONLY ONE!

1
2
SH
UP
2
1
DOK
HUH ?!

HEY HEY HEY!!! YOU WANT HELP?! WELL, DO YA?!
HEY HEY HEY HEY
MAKE UP YER MIND!!!
YIPES! I LIKED THE FIRST ONE BETTER!

SHUP

SORRY! IT'S OKAY! TAKE YOUR TIME!
WHOA! ANOTHER ONE!

WELL, UM, YOU SEE...
I DROPPED MY GAME IN A PUDDLE–

I WASN'T ASKIN' YOU!!!
SHUP
I WAS ASKIN' HIROTA!!!
DOOM
WHOA! YOU AGAIN?!

SORRY, IT'S JUST HOW WE'RE STACKED...
ER, RIGHT. HEH.
ME ...?
UM, WELL, COULD YOU FIX NOBORU'S GAME FOR ME, THEN?
That's how I do it, right?

NOD
BUT OF COURSE!
Thanks!
AL-RIGHT!

SHUP

SNIFF
WHOA! THERE'S ANOTHER ONE!
4

MAYBE WE CAN DO IT, MAYBE WE CAN'T.
THERE'S LOTS WE CAN'T DO, REALLY...
4

WE'RE DOOMED!
NO WE'RE NOT! THERE'S ONE MORE CUP!

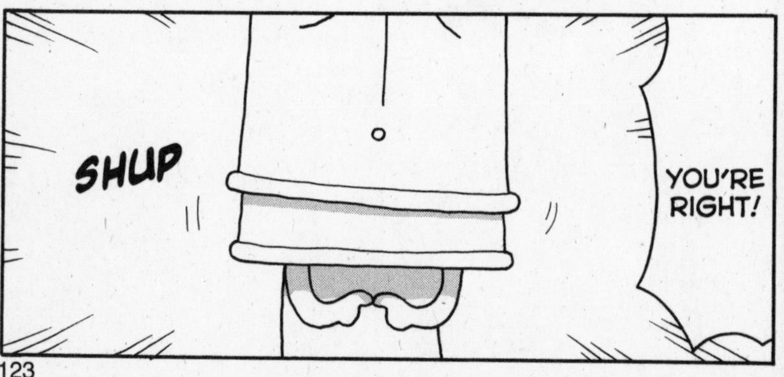
YOU'RE RIGHT!
SHUP

5

WOOF
WOOF
WOOF
NAH, WE'RE DOOMED. SORRY!
IT'S NOT YOUR FAULT ...

CHAPTER 13

Five Kinds of Help

CUP 1!
TAH!
I'M THE LEADER!

HEY
HEY
CUP 2!
I'M THE GRUMPY OLD MAN!
HEY
CUP 3!
There, there...
I'M THE CARING MOTHERLY CUP!

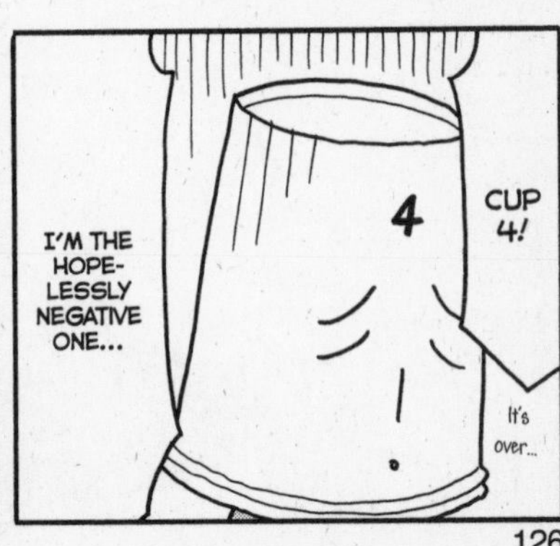
CUP 4!
I'M THE HOPE-LESSLY NEGATIVE ONE...
It's over...

WOOF WOOF
CUP 5!
AND OUR PET, CUPOOCH!

HIROTA'S HELPERS
TA DAAAH
WE'RE THE FIVE CUPS!
ALL TOGETH- ER...
THE FIVE CUPS

HIROTA RECYCLED US DURING HIS VACATION!
SO YOU'RE RECYCLED ROBOTS, TOO?
YES!
THAT'S COOL... I GUESS.
STACK
STACK

VACATION ?!
WAIT! I REMEMBER!
You do?

VACATION
SERVICE AREA
SHOP
TOILET

SPLOOSH

QUIK CARD
I COULD GO FOR SOME WATER!

HELP YOURSELF, IT'S FREE!
WATER
HOT TEA
UM...
WHERE'RE THE CUPS ...?

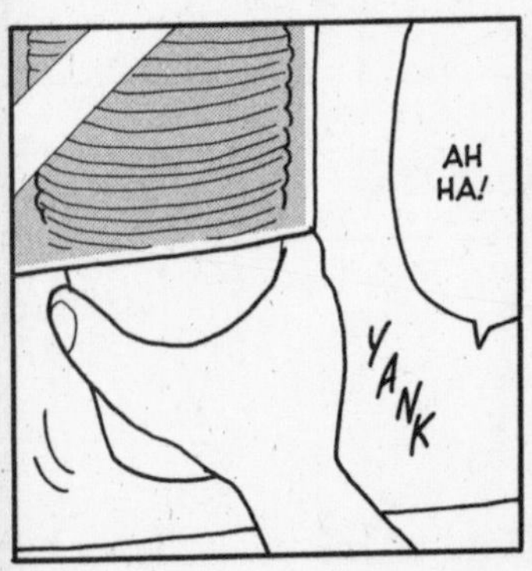
AH HA!
YANK

KER
SHUK
Five cups at once

TOSS
PAPER CUPS ONLY

What do I do now?!
HIROTA! WE'RE LEAVING!
WAAH! OH NO!
'KAY, MOM!

YEAH... I REMEMBER...
UM, GREAT STORY.
YOU DIDN'T EVEN USE THEM!

SO! CAN YOU FIX NOBORU'S GAME?!
SNAP
LEAVE IT TO US!

IF THERE'S ONE THING WE'VE GOT...
IT'S TEAMWORK!!!
1
SWITCH!!!
2
SHUP

COME ON, YOU LOUSY THING!!!
QUIT BEIN' LAZY!!!

GET TO WORK!!!
WORK!!!
WORK!!!!

GRUMBLE
...

SWITCH!!!
SHUP

LET'S TRY HITTING IT...
WHAP
WHAP
THIS OUGHTA DO IT!
...

SWITCH!!
SHUP

HMMMM
OH... I'VE NEVER BEEN GOOD AT FIXING THINGS...
I'LL PROBABLY MAKE THINGS WORSE, SO I'M NOT EVEN GOING TO TRY.

SWITCH!!
WOOF
WOOF
SWITCH!!
WOOF

AND NOW FOR A MAGIC TRICK!
I KNEW IT!

ZZUP
...REPORTING!!
ZOIK
WHOA! PET CAME TO!
1
2
3
4
5

SOMETHING WRONG?
EVERYTHING!

I SEE...!
MIND IF I TAKE A LOOK?
SURE, GO AHEAD.

THE SCREEN IS RUINED!
DING
YOU JUST NEED A REPLACE-MENT!

HEY!
WOW!!
THAT'S NOT BAD, PET!
...

FIRST, YOU REMOVE THE OLD SCREEN...
KRIK
POK
FLAP
FLAP
THEN SWITCH IN THE NEW ONE!

NEW SCREEN

THAT'S WAY TOO BIG!!
...
HUH? WELL, A LITTLE ...

MORE THAN A LITTLE !!!
NO PROBLEM, IT'S SUP-PORTED!
ARE YOU SURE?!
KLIK

VROOM
'01"42
'01"38
TA DA!!!
WOW! IT'S A BIG-SCREEN GAME NOW!!
29-INCH SCREEN

VROOM
VROOM

MY ARMS ARE GETTING TIRED!!!!
Uh...

NOW, FOR A MAGIC TRICK!

CHAPTER 14

Plaz About the House

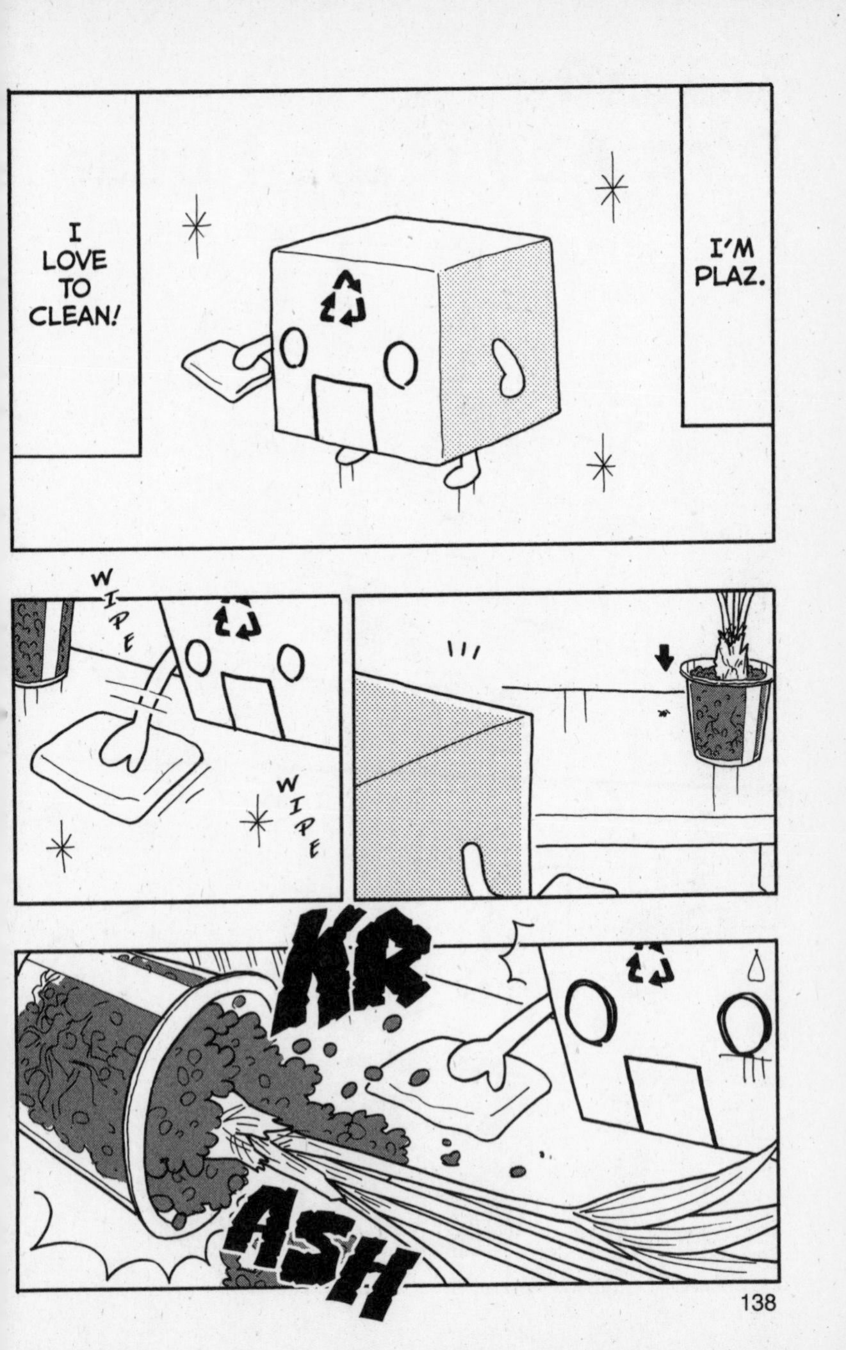
I'M PLAZ.
I LOVE TO CLEAN!
WIPE
WIPE
KR
ASH

TMP TMP
TMP
...

EEEK!
THUMP
SPLOOSH
WHEE!
DRIP
HEY!
DRIP
DRIP

PET! HELP US!!!
NOBORU NEEDS ME!

WOOSH
I'LL COME TOO!

...
CHIPS

MOP
MOP
PLAZ IS ON THE JOB!
MANGA

IN HIS FREE TIME ...
KLIK
KLIK
KLIK
HE LIKES TO UPGRADE HIMSELF!

Latest Plaz Data
June 1 - Plaz Version 3.0 J
June 2 - Plaz Version 3.1 J
June 3 - Plaz Version 3.12 J
June 4 - Plaz Version 3.2 J
June 5 - Plaz Version 3.22 J
EVERY DAY, HE DOWNLOADS NEW PLAZ DATA!

ACK! A NEW VERSION!
I'VE GOTTA DOWNLOAD THIS!

OH NO! WAIT!!!
THAT WAS PET'S DATA!!!

WAY TO GO, PLAZ!
TMP
TMP
Whee!
TMP

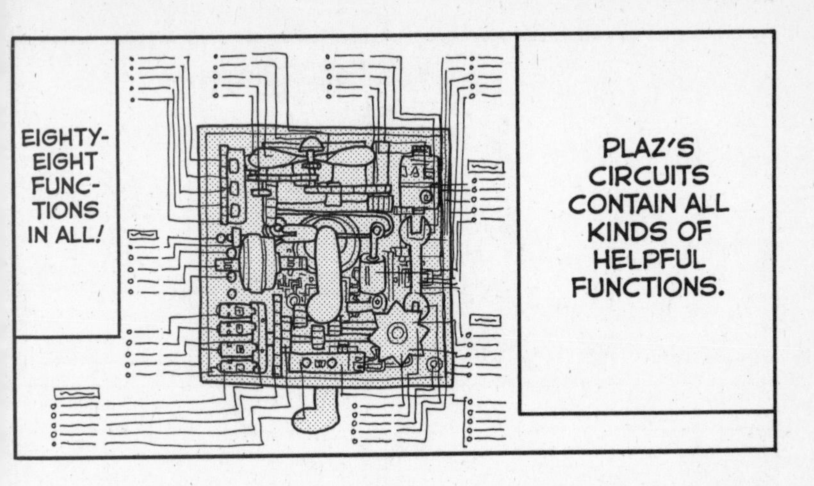
PLAZ'S CIRCUITS CONTAIN ALL KINDS OF HELPFUL FUNCTIONS.
EIGHTY-EIGHT FUNCTIONS IN ALL!

PLAZ, CAN YOU PLAY THIS FOR ME?
SURE!
KLIK
HE CAN PLAY CDS!

PLAY THIS ONE NEXT!
OKAY...
Yum, yum, in my dish!
Blup blup goes the fish!

HEY PLAZ, CAN YOU PLAY THIS ONE?
Mine too!
OKAY...
Buzz, buzz, buzz go the bees—
WAY TO GO, PLAZ!
88 FUNCTIONS AND THEY ONLY USE THE CD PLAYER.

CHAPTER 15 The Haunted House

MORNING

CHAPTER 15

The Haunted House

LINE UP HERE, PLEASE!
GULP
GULP
GULP

ARE WE REALLY GOING IN?!
GULP GULP
YES! I LOVE HAUNTED HOUSES!
What fun!
GULP GULP

Waaaah! That was scary!
ACK...

I DUNNO...
IT'S OK!
YES? HELLO?
GULP GULP

OH, HI! WOW, LONG TIME NO TALK!
HANG ON A SECOND, IT'S A LITTLE NOISY–
I'LL JUST GET TO A QUIET SPOT.
HUH?!

.....

NEXT IN LINE?
TRANCE
UUUUM...

WHAT DO WE DO, DAD?!
GULP
GULP
I-I'M NOT REALLY A FAN OF HAUNTED HOUSES EITHER.
HUG
GULP

IN YOU GO!!!
SHOVE
H-HEY!

GULP
GULP
THIS WAY
SHIVER
SHIVER

BOO!

AAAAUGH!!!
BOING
...

HELP!!!
HELP!!!

YOU CALLED AND I HAVE COME! IT'S PET!

HUH? PET?
WHO'S PET?

MY HELPER ROBOT!!!
Oh yeah!
HUH?

WHAT'S WRONG, NOBORU?
PET
AAAH

WAAAAH!
ZOIK
WHAT? WHAT IS IT ?!
VWIP
VWIP
AAAAAAUGH!!

TMP
TMP TMP
TMP
WAAAAH!
WAAAAAH!!!

TMP TMP TMP
EEEEK!
WAAAAAUGH!
TMP TMP

Waaah!
...WAIT A SECOND !!!

WHAT ARE YOU RUNNING FROM?!
UM ...
I dunno.

AND WHY ARE YOU DRESSED LIKE THAT ?!
OH! THIS?

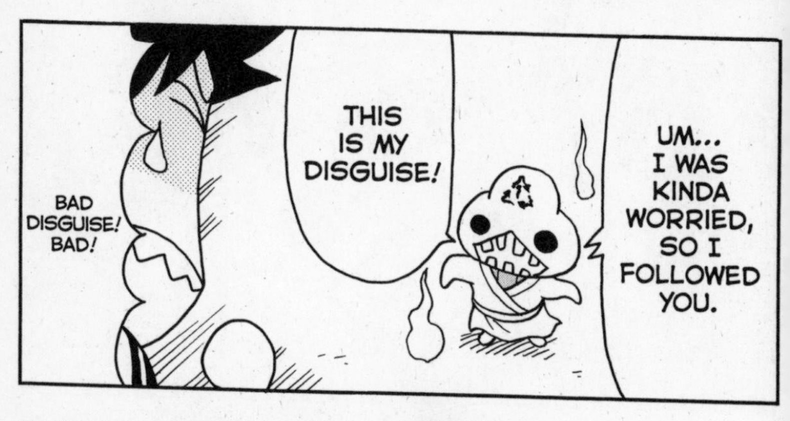
UM... I WAS KINDA WORRIED, SO I FOLLOWED YOU.
THIS IS MY DISGUISE!
BAD DISGUISE! BAD!

BUT I GUESS YOU RECOGNIZED ME.
Oh well...
YEAH, YOU CAN CHANGE BACK.

SAY GOOD-BYE TO THE SPECIAL HAUNTED HOUSE VERSION OF PET!
SEE YA!

KRREEEK

KRREEEK

VWWW
WING

THERE! GOOD AS NEW!
TA DA
NEXT TIME, LEAVE OUT THE HEAD TWISTING THING.

WHAT? YOU CAN'T FIND THE EXIT?!
OK! I'VE GOT JUST THE THING!

FWAP
MY HAUNTED HOUSE MAP!
WHOA!
THAT'S COOL!

TA-DA!!!
AMAZING!!!
ENTRANCE
EXIT
AND HERE'S THE EXIT!
HE'S RIGHT!

SO, WHERE ARE WE NOW?
Everything's going to be OK!
UM...

I DUNNO.
ZOMG
WHA—?!

WHAT GOOD DOES THAT DO US?!
HELP!!!!

CHAPTER 16

Let's Get Out of Here!

PET HAS COME TO RESCUE NOBORU'S FAMILY FROM THE HAUNTED HOUSE...
SHIVER
GULP
SHIVER
GULP
Waaaah.

A DEAD END!!!
Whaaa—?!
Don't say "dead"
NOW THEY'RE ALL STUCK!

TELL ME YOU BROUGHT A FLASH-LIGHT!
You're a robot, right?
OH YEAH!

PET LIGHT ...
ON!

CLIC K

CLICK

ARRRRGH!!!
THAT'S EVEN SCARIER!!
Mwa ha ha.
Turn it off!

PLAZ?!
HEY GUYS!

WHY DOES YOUR WHOLE HEAD HAVE TO LIGHT UP?!
And the creepy laugh?!
THAT'S THE ONLY LIGHT I BROUGHT...

WAAAAAAAAUGH!!!

It's the faceless Plaz!!!
HUH?

OOPS!
FORGOT TO DRAW MY FACE!
SQUEEK

TA DA
WHAT'S WRONG, GUYS?

HEY, IT'S ALU!
AND SHE'S NORMAL! THANK GOOD-NESS!

POK

WAAAAAUGH!!!!

HUH?
MUST HAVE A LOOSE SCREW ...
SQUEEK
SQUEEK

HELP!!!
TMP TMP TMP
TMP TMP TMP

HELP?!
I'LL HELP YOU!

TINY TIN!!!
VWIP
VWIP
VWIP
Tiny who?!
WHERE ARE YOU?!
VWIP

RATTLE
RATTLE
RATTLE
RATTLE

HUH
MUH

AAAAAH!!!
TMP TMP
PEH! PEH!
THEY SHOULD CHANGE THAT WATER!

MY TIME HAS COME!!!
TA
DA
P-2 REPOR–

-TING !!!
KER
POW

SNIFF
SNIFF
SNIFF
SNIFF

ZOIK !!
SNIFF
SNIFF
WHA-WHA-WHAT'S THAT?

SHUP

Untie me! Untie me!
WAAAAH! STAY AWAY!!!

HELP!!!
Grrrk.
PLEASE! GUYS?
AWU TIED ME TOO TIGHT!
TSK.
Waah!
THEY'RE NO HELP AT ALL!

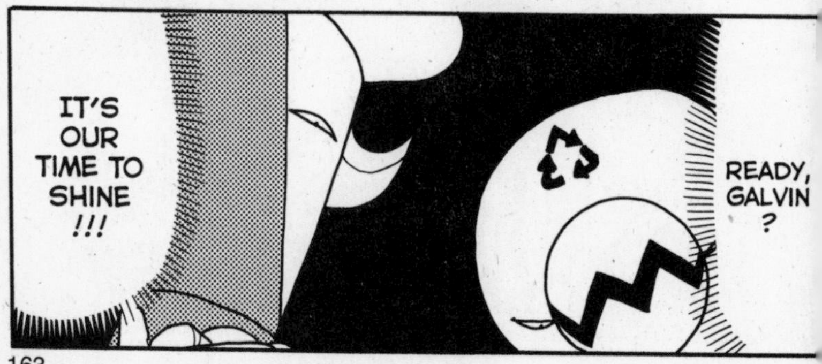
READY, GALVIN?
IT'S OUR TIME TO SHINE!!!

FLAP
FLAP
FLAP
WE'LL HELP YOU!!!
THE CAN CREW

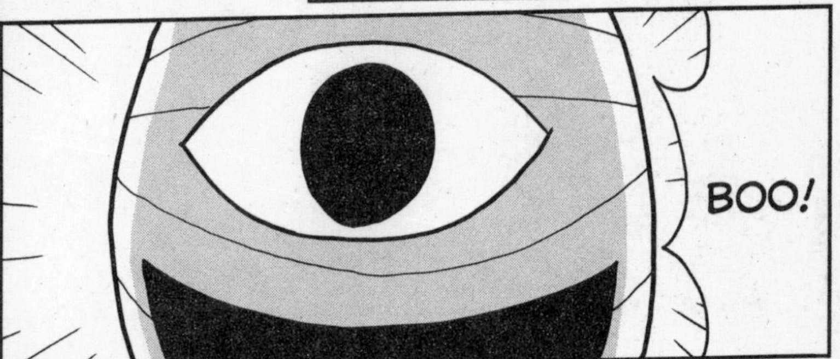
BOO!

BONK

ZOIK

ZONG

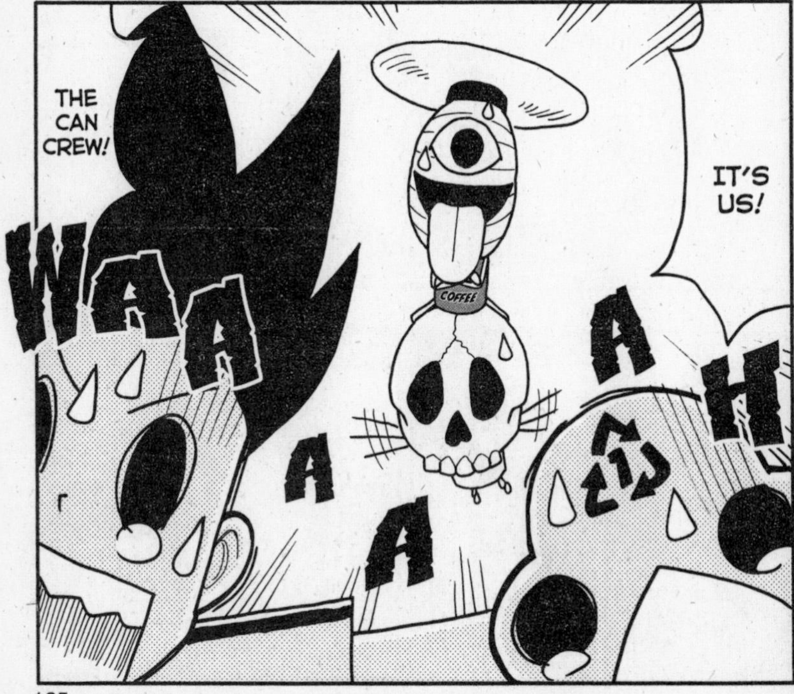
IT'S US!
THE CAN CREW!
WAAAAAH

BONK

WE'RE OUT!!!
WE DID IT!

EXIT
WHA-?!
HAVE FUN?

I CAN'T BELIEVE YOU WENT WITHOUT ME!
WE'RE GOING THROUGH AGAIN!

HUH?!

AAAAAAAAAAH

CHAPTER 17

A Day with PET

PET DOES NOT LIKE NOBORU'S BABY BROTHER, HIKARU.
NOBORU'S BABY BROTHER HIKARU, AGE 3.

WHY?
PEB! PEB!

IT'S PET, GOT IT?! PET!
OOH?
PEB?
BECAUSE HE CALLS PET FUNNY NAMES.

PET AND HIKARU ARE NOT FRIENDS.
VROOOOM
...
WHY?

TRANS-FORM!!
POK
POK

SUPER TWAIN FORM!!
GO!
...
BECAUSE HE LIKES TO TRANS-FORM PET HIMSELF.

PET AND HIKARU? NOT SO MUCH.
WHY ?

WHERE'S MY BOTTLE ?!
HUH?
BECAUSE HE LOSES PET'S BOTTLE.

WRONG BOTTLE !!!
AND PUTS THE WRONG ONE ON.

ENERGY

PET IS NOT HIKARU'S NUMBER ONE FAN.
WHY?

COOL!
ZOMG
...
BECAUSE HIKARU LIKES TO DRAW. ON PET.

PET JUST DOES NOT LIKE HIKARU.
PET!
Help us!!!
WHY?

SNAG
PET REPORT–

NO WEAVE!
B-BUT NOBORU NEEDS–
BE-CAUSE HE DOESN'T LET PET GO.

HELP ME!!!

OK!
LEAVE IT TO PLAZ!

HUH?!
Wheee!
ZOOM
NOW'S MY CHANCE!

PLAZ DOES NOT LIKE HIKARU.
CAN YOU GUESS WHY?
Pwad! Pwad!

CHAPTER 18 The Haunted School

CHAPTER 18
The Haunted School

DA DAA

WAAAAH!
CREEPY!

GO RIGHT IN!
THANKS!
Whew!

BETTER BRING A FLASH-LIGHT.
THANKS!

HUH?
TOK TOK

...SO, WHERE'S YOUR ROOM?
TOK TOK
THIRD FLOOR. ALL THE WAY IN THE BACK...
SHIVER

ZOK

WHAT'RE WE GONNA DO?!
G-G-GO HOME!
SHIVER
SHIVER

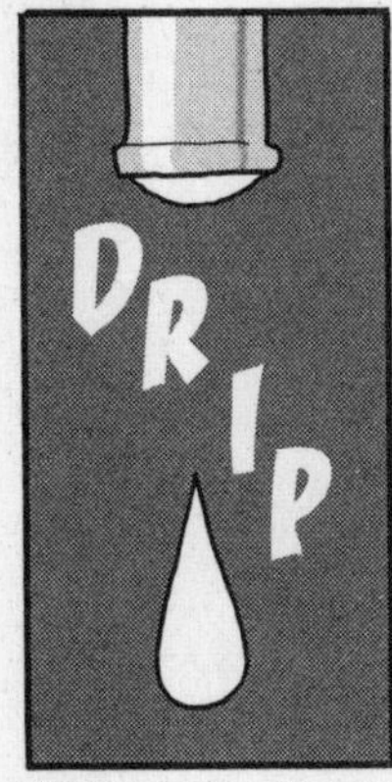
DRIP

ZO
WAAAAAUGH!!!
IK

DRIP
IT'S JUST WATER!

WH-WHY DON'T YOU CALL PET?
AAAA....
G-G-GOOD IDEA!
Dad, don't do that with your light.

PUH-PUH-PET ...?
SHIVER
SHIVER
PAH-PAH-PET !!!

TA DAAA
Papa
REPORT-
ING!
PAPA
PET!

WHAT?!
PAPA PET
Papa

I'M
PAPA
PET! OR
PAPET,
FOR
SHORT!
Papa
REPORT-
ING!
VERY
FUNNY,
PET!
That's...
not much
shorter.

FWAP
QUIT
FOOLIN'
AROUND
!!
We need
your help—

HU
NH
Papa

Papa

...
PAPA PET IS POWERLESS WITHOUT HIS GLASSES.
PAT
MY GLASSES! MY GLASSES!
Papa
PAT

WHAT'S THE BIG IDEAR?!
YOU NUMB-SKULL!!
GRR GRR
Papa
I GUESS YOU AREN'T PET...

PAPA PET IS A PET JUST FOR DAD!
Recycled Robots for the Whole Family!
PET helps Noboru
Other PETs
Papa
Momma
Papa PET / Helps Dad
Momma PET / Helps Mom
FAMILY SIZE!
ALL IN THE FAMILY!
Papa

WHAAA-?! REALLY?!
FOR ME?
WHILE SUPPLIES LAST!

I left my homework in the classroom...
Can you go get it?
Papa

SO, ER, WHAT DO YOU NEED AGAIN?
Wow, my own robot!
OH... RIGHT!

I left my homework in the classroom...
Can you go get it?
Papa

EH?! EH?!
Papa
WHAT'S THAT, SONNY?
UM, ER...

NO! I DON'T DO HELPING, GOT IT?!
No way!
Papa
WHAT?! I THOUGHT YOU WERE A HELPER ROBOT?!

WHO TOLD YOU THAT NON-SENSE?!
When? Where?
Papa

I DUNNO, I JUST THOUGHT—
WELL, YOU THOUGHT WRONG!!!
I mean, c'mon...

I'M AN ADVICE ROBOT!!
ADVICE
Papa
AN ADVICE ROBOT...?

WHAT'S AN ADVICE ROBOT?
A ROBOT THAT GIVES ADVICE!
Papa

WHAA—?! JUST ADVICE?!
What good is that?
JUST ADVICE!

PAPA PET'S GOOD ADVICE
HERE'S MY ADVICE FOR YOU!!!
STOP BEING SUCH A SCAREDY-CAT!!!
Papa

THAT IS ALL.
WHA-?!
THAT'S IT?!
TOK TOK
Pa

NO THROWIN' OUT THOSE POTATO PEELS! YOU CAN USE THOSE IN THE SALAD!
HUH? WHO ARE YOU?
Momma PET's advice

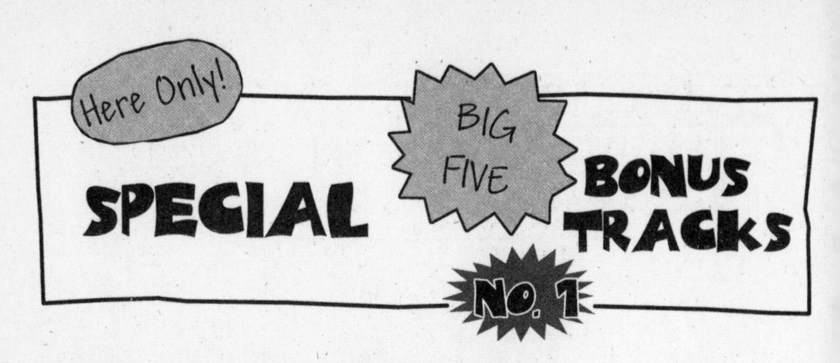

CONNECT THE DOTS! (BEGINNER LEVEL) DRAW A LINE BETWEEN THE NUMBERS 1 THROUGH 58 IN ORDER TO REVEAL THE HIDDEN PICTURE!!!

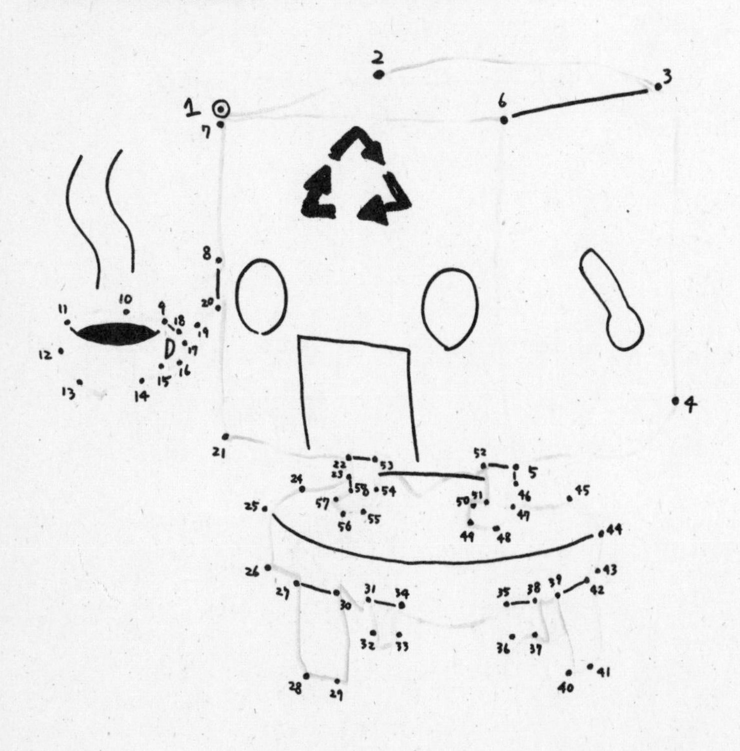

ANSWER ON PAGE 190!

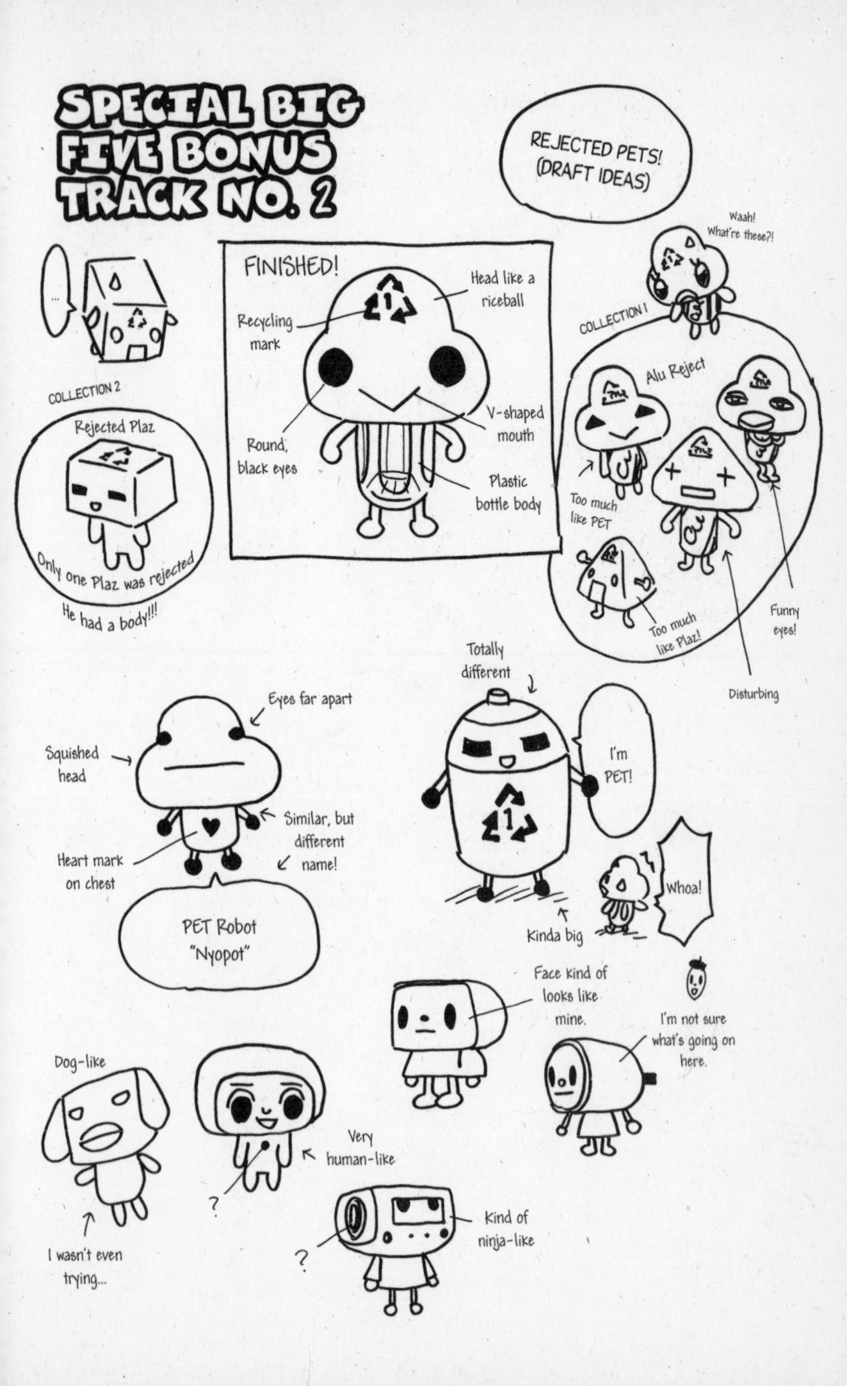
SPECIAL BIG FIVE BONUS TRACK NO. 2
REJECTED PETS! (DRAFT IDEAS)
...
FINISHED!
Recycling mark
Head like a riceball
Round, black eyes
V-shaped mouth
Plastic bottle body
Waah! What're these?!
COLLECTION 1
Alu Reject
Too much like PET
Too much like Plaz!
Funny eyes!
Disturbing
COLLECTION 2
Rejected Plaz
Only one Plaz was rejected
He had a body!!!
Totally different
I'm PET!
Whoa!
Kinda big
Eyes far apart
Squished head
Similar, but different name!
Heart mark on chest
PET Robot "Nyopot"
Face kind of looks like mine.
I'm not sure what's going on here.
Dog-like
I wasn't even trying...
Very human-like
?
Kind of ninja-like
?

SPECIAL BIG FIVE BONUS NO. 3

The Tools

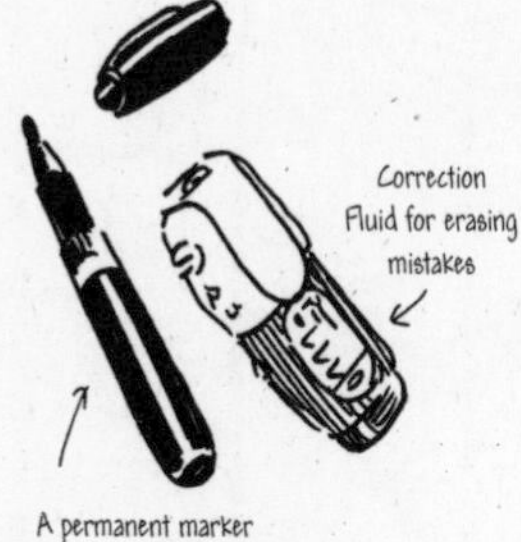

FROM PAPER TO COMPUTER

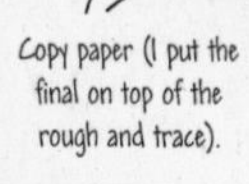

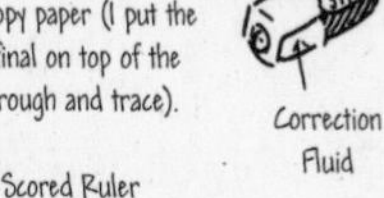

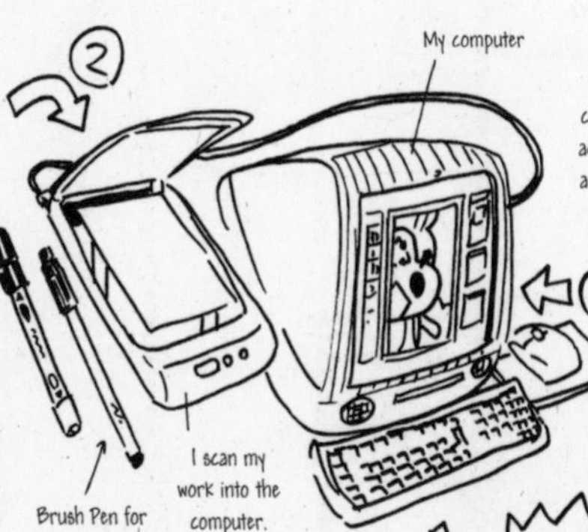

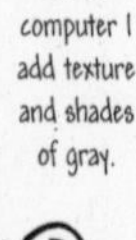

SPECIAL BIG FIVE BONUS TRACK NO. 4

FIND THE RECYCLE ROBOT THAT'S RIGHT FOR YOU! PICK A NUMBER BETWEEN 1 AND 7, AND START AT THAT LINE. ALWAYS TRACE DOWN, AND WHENEVER YOU COME TO A LINE THAT GOES LEFT OR RIGHT, YOU HAVE TO TAKE THAT LINE!

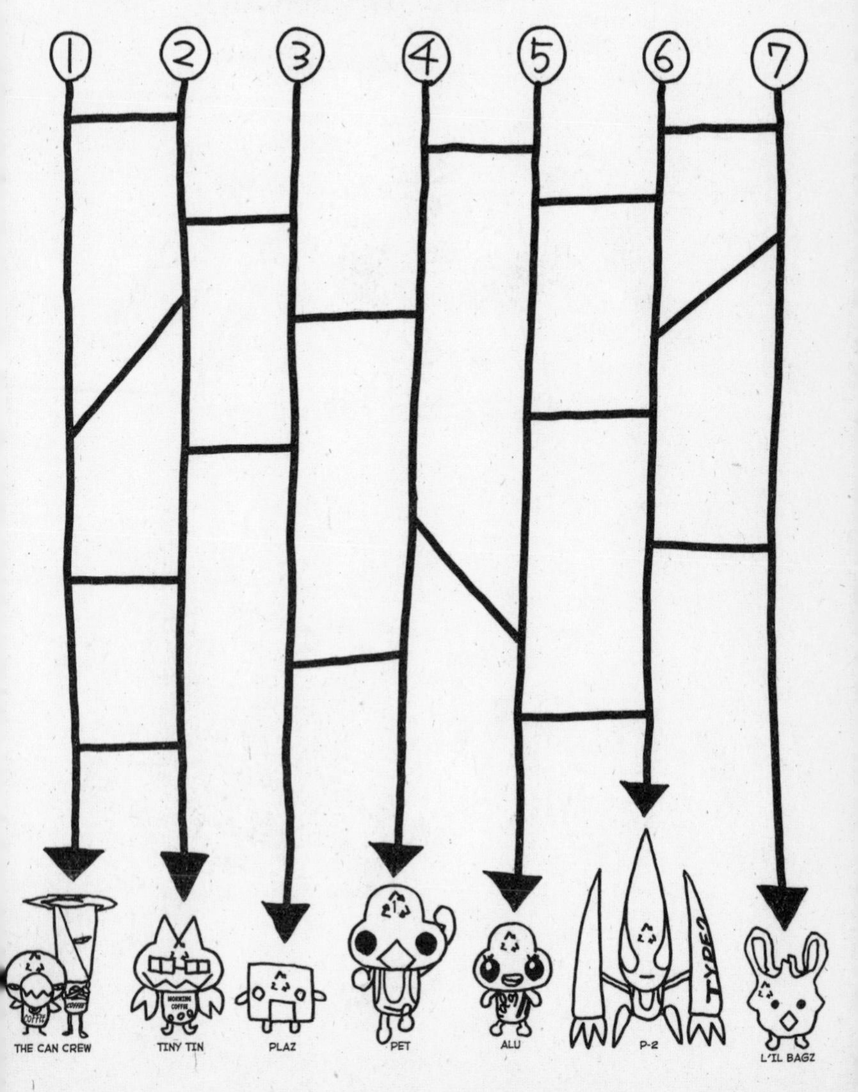

SPECIAL BIG FIVE BONUS TRACK NO. 5

CONNECT THE DOTS! (EXPERT LEVEL)
CONNECT THE DOTS FROM 1 TO 111 TO REVEAL THE HIDDEN PICTURE!

ANSWER ON PAGE 190!

Special Bonus Track Answers

A Note About Recycling Symbols

In Japan, where ***Leave It to PET!*** originated, recycling is an important part of everyday life. While we only have one symbol ♻ that's used on most things that are recyclable in the United States, in Japan, just about every material has a symbol of its own. For example:

PET

The symbol for recyclable polyethylene terephthalate – the kind of plastic most plastic bottles are made of – can be found all over the world. Sometimes it appears with the word **"PETE"** instead of **"PET."**

This is the symbol for recyclable **aluminum**.

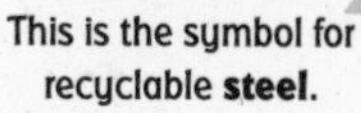

This is the symbol for recyclable **steel**.

This is the symbol for recyclable **plastic other than PET bottles**.

Coming Soon!

The hijinks continue in volume three of

Leave It to PET!

The robots keep coming and the adventures get more outrageous in this volume of *Leave It to PET!* PET, Plaz and Alu super-charge their powers, PET becomes a doctor, and the whole team battles an out-of-control chicken?

Expect the unexpected in volume 3 of *Leave It to PE*